The Adventures

Book 7

Charley Cooper
'And The Fractured Gene'

V. G. Walker

The Adventures of Charley Cooper

(Books 1-14)

Charley Cooper's Time-Out

Charley Cooper – Time-Traveller

Charley Cooper - Double Time

Charley Cooper - Out Of Time

Charley Cooper - Over Time

Charley Cooper - Future Time

Charley Cooper And The Fractured-Gene

Charley Cooper – Lost In Time

Charley Cooper And The New Generation

New Times

New Threat

Aftermath

Other-Time Delivers

'Nemesis'
(An Ending)

'Legacy'
The Final Adventure

Dedicated to:

All the children I have taught…

and possibly their own children

&

To Barrie, Tom and Kate

as always

The Characters

Earth-Time

Charley Cooper

Mum - Jenny Cooper

Gran - Margaret Cooper (Pugh)

Dad - Henry John Cooper

Colin Stubbs

Mum - Patricia Stubbs

Sister - Jane Stubbs

Dad - Simon Stubbs

Mr Harris - Headteacher

Mr. Trimble - History teacher

Mrs Spencer - Mathematics/Numeracy

Lee Kelly - pupil

Stuart 'Stu' Hunter - pupil

Mr. Stephens - Teacher PE

Margery - Dinner lady

Tom Bailey - United's Scout

Philip Faversham

Felicity Albright

Stephanie Mason (Nee Bennett)

Sarah Sutton

Leanne Colin's girlfriend

The Cooper's

23, Starch Lane, Flexington

Gran

Wisteria Cottage, Flexington

The Stubbs

4, Primrose Crescent, Flexington

New Characters in 'Earth-Time'

Ben Read - footballer

Leanne - girlfriend

Alec Jones – United's physiotherapist

Ethan Faversham

<u>Other-Time</u>

SAM - Sebastian Aloysius Mountelbaine

Abigail Drew - Featherstone

Arnold

Pogs - the dog

'Dawson' - Tom Dawson

Bill Steadman - Dawson's Security Team

Danny - Dawson's Security Team

Patrick Blackthorne

Anastasia Nikolaev

Victor Savage

Peterson

Mickey - Michael Flood

Bestie - Connel Bestwood

Delia Faversham

Dorcas Faversham

Florence Faversham

Dorothy Pinkton

Toby Thompson

Chapters

Introduction

Charley Cooper… like his grandparents and his father before him… carries a *'special gene'*.
This allows him to move between *'Earth-Time'* and *'Other-Time'*.
"*Other-Time'* is just a moment away… a mere *'step to the side'* from time, here on Earth.
Here you can develop individual *'abilities'* within *'teams'*… in *'sectors'*… with other *'Double-Timers'*.
Charley is in <u>S</u>ebastian <u>A</u>loysius <u>M</u>ountelbaine - SAM's - *'team', in 'Sector 4'* of *'Other-Time'*.
SAM is Charley's grandfather and the *'team'* have become like a second family to him, now.

Charley had lost his father at the age of seven.
Henry John Cooper had died a hero in Afghanistan, saving the life of another *'Other-Time' 'team'* member.
He was a hero… in both *'Times'*… but then he'd always been a hero to Charley.
Charley's mum had died when he was fourteen… of a broken heart.
She could cope no longer, without her Henry.

'Gran' had always been there for Charley.

Having returned and settled in *'Earth-Time'...* to *be there* for her family... for Henry and Jenny and Charley... she was his, constant, support.
In *'Other-Time'* Gran had been known as Nanny Peg – by its younger members and as just 'Peg' by, such as, SAM and Arnold.

As well as Charley, within SAM's *'team'* were Abi, Arnold, Dorcas, Bestie and Pogs - the dog.
All had their own special *'abilities'*:
Abi, like SAM, was a *'mind-reader'* and *'empath'*;
Arnold was a *'shape-changer'...* which was unusual... even for *'Other-Time'*;
Dorcas *'heard'* voices and, at times, *'saw'* the future... in *'visions'*;
Bestie could *'read-minds'...* had an *'Inner-Eye'...* that allowed him to *'find'* anyone (even when they didn't wish to be found) and was capable of moving at *'high speed'* and jumping extremely high, too.

That just leaves Pogs – the huge, grey, shaggy, boisterous dog, who *'spoke'* in the minds of the *'team'*.
The *bane* of Arnold's life, he was always tripping Arnold up. And, because Arnold would always be shouting 'that pesky dogs at it again!'... (or some such exclamation) as he fell over him... time and time

again… 'Pesky dogs' got shortened, eventually, to Pogs.

Charley was also an 'empath' (was empathic), like his gran.
He could pick up on people's *feelings* and always knew when something was *wrong*… when people had *negative* or *ill intentions* towards *'Other-Time'*.
He was also a *'traveller'*.
Though it had never been known before in *'Other-Time'* – Charley could *'travel through time'*.
He had *'travelled'* back in time, several times now, but this only happened at a time of great need.
He had also *'travelled'*… once… into the future, when intoxicated on *'Travel-Juice'*!

In *'Earth-Time'* Colin was Charley's best friend.
Just seventeen, like Charley, he now played for 'United's' under 21 Team or, at times, the reserve team.
Colin had always loved football… well he 'lived' it!
Football, food and fun were his passions. Colin was very uncomplicated.
At fourteen Colin had *trialled* for *his* team and he had never looked back. He had subbed, for the 1st Team, on his seventeenth birthday… and nearly scored!

Though Colin had always hated school, he had done better than expected in his exams and had entered the Sixth Form College with Charley – though this, of course, took a backseat to football.

Charley, however, was always eager to learn. Specialising in Science - he was enjoying every minute of his college course.

Now, with the first year of 'A' levels over, he knew he would soon have to make some, important, decisions, about his future.
Should he enter *'Other-Time'* permanently… go to university and have a career in *'Earth-Time'…* or just continue his *'double-life'*?
Colin and Gran were here in *'Earth-Time'* but Abi, SAM and the *'team'* were also his family, now.

Finding Danny

'Other-Time' had been under threat for some years from a man named Patrick Blackthorne.
He had carried a *'fractured-gene'* but now, with Blackthorne finally defeated *'Other-Time'* and its *'teams'* could relax… at long last!
However, records were discovered that showed Blackthorne had a son who, they believed, also carried the *'fractured-gene'*.

It appeared that Blackthorne was unaware of his son's existence.
He'd been hidden by a loving mother… kept un-aware… and safely away from Blackthorne's evil influence.
Now remarried, Danny Mason's mother – Stephanie - had brought her son up, well, and in a caring and loving environment.
In fact Danny had become a well-liked and trusted member of *'Other-Time's Security Team'…* run by Tom Dawson.
He had been both trusted and valued but that was before he and *'Other-Time'* had learnt the truth!

Danny Mason was Blackthorne's son…

He carried the same *'fractured-gene'* and everything had changed!

Danny sat, alone, thinking.
He couldn't get his head around all that had happened!
One day he was a loving son and boyfriend to Sarah in *'Earth-Time'* and had a great job… which he'd loved… with *'Other-Times' Security-Team'* but then…
Now – he was in hiding! He was being *'hunted'* and by the very *'team'* he'd worked for!
He hadn't known he was Blackthorne's son… or that he'd carried this *'gene'*!

It was so, very, unfair!
Danny had done nothing wrong!
But – Danny had determination and the sense of *self-preservation* within him… to survive this.

Charley sat in with the *'team'* as they discussed their next moves.
The *'Security-Teams'*, under Dawson, were *'scanning'* for Danny's DNA , in *'Earth-Time'* and *'Other-Time'*, without success.
SAM's *'team'* and Dawson's *'teams'* were very uncomfortable at having to hunt down a man who, a

few days before, had been a trusted colleague… and a friend.

However, the *'fractured-gene'* was a threat to *'Other-Time'* … or it had been.
It had passed from Blackthorne to Danny and from Philip Faversham to Delia, Dorcas' twin sister, but not to Dorcas.
Now, *'they'* were all gone. The Faversham's in a fire and Blackthorne destroyed out in the *'void'*… blasted into *'Out-of-Time'*… and oblivion.
Danny was now the only *'carrier'*.

"We've had no luck … as yet!" Dawson sighed.
"No sightings, no traces from the *'scanners'* and no ideas. The *'Earth-Time'* *'team'* say that his mother and girlfriend have still had no contact … and they are, naturally, very worried!"

Bill Steadman, Dawson's right-hand-man, remained silent.
He and Danny were good friends. As he was Dawson's right-hand-man… so Danny was his.

Abi and Arnold were Danny's friends, too.
Danny had helped save Abi when she'd been abducted by Blackthorne's protégé, Victor Savage.

Savage had been one of Blackthorne's *'team'*
members... hand-picked for his ruthless and self-
centred qualities... from what had then been *'Sector
12'*.
This *'sector'* no longer existed and was now the site
of The Lake.

SAM, however, had *'Other-Time'* to safeguard.
He had to put *'Other-Time'* first... as did Tom Dawson
... but this didn't mean they enjoyed what was
happening.

Charley watched... and listened.
His *'feelings'* told him that he must try and help
Danny. *How* he might help... he wasn't sure... as
yet?
But Charley trusted his *'feelings'*.

Charley Tells Bill His Idea

Charley watched Bill *'step-out'* from the meeting, though nothing had been resolved.
When the *'team'* broke up, Charley, also, *'stepped-out'…* and found Bill.

"Oh! Hi, Charley.
What are you thinking?"
"That someone has to find Danny… and help him. Not sure how, as yet, though… I admit."

"Just what I've been thinking. He must be in a real state.
He's a good bloke… and a good mate, Charley.

"Bestie wasn't at the meeting… he's still in *'Earth-Time'*… but I thought we could try his *'inner-eye'* to pinpoint Danny's whereabouts.
I thought they'd have thought about that, before, but, since *we have* …"
Bill smiled… and together they *'stepped-out'* and *'stepped-in'* to Connel Bestwood's home.
Felicity Bestwood… once Felicity Albright of *'Other-Time'*… showed Charley and Bill into the garden

where Bestie was still revising, for a final exam at his private school.

"Hi, Charley… Bill," he said… happy to be distracted from his notes for a while. "How are things going?"

Charley put Bestie in the picture… and he was only too pleased to try and help.

Although he couldn't remember ever meeting Danny, Bill provided a 'likeness' from 'Other-Time' and Bestie closed his eyes and concentrated… for a long time.

Charley and Bill waited.

When Bestie, finally, opened his eyes, he had nothing for them.

"He's not in 'Earth-Time'… I'm sure. I tried 'Other-Time', too… Nothing! And I 'feel' I should be able to find him."

"Ok, thanks, Bestie." Charley said, as he was about to 'step-out'. "It was worth a try!"

Charley nodded at Bill, who also thanked Bestie, as they 'stepped-out'.

"That's it!

I had a 'feeling'…" Charley stated as they 'stepped-in' together to Bill's place.

Bill looked at him.

"You thinking…?" Bill began.

"He's *'Out-of-Time'*... has to be! Where else could he get *completely* away from us... from everything... to think?"

"You're right, Charley!"

Bill thought for a time, before adding, "He, just, might have done that."

But Bill was troubled...

"Listen, Charley..." he said slowly, "...there is something... somewhere... I shouldn't talk about. Only one or two of us know. Perhaps I should do this... I mean... try and find Danny... alone."

Charley saw the point.

"I understand but... if this is where Danny's gone... the *'team'* will *have* to know about it... soon!"

Charley studied Bill.

"You've got another *'holding-cell'*... a new *'location'*!"

Bill sighed at Charley's, *educated guess*.

"Well, since you've guessed... I suppose it'll be ok."

Charley could see that Bill was, obviously, disturbed by what he was about to do.

"I'll have to tell Tom, though, Charley," he said. "... when we get back?"

"Exactly!" agreed Charley.

Both *'holding-locations'*... that had previously held Blackthorne and Victor Savage in *'Out-of-Time'*... had been destroyed by Blackthorne, himself.

Victor Savage had died in the first explosion… which was just what Blackthorne had intended. The second explosion had been designed to kill SAM and the *'team'*, at source, but was of such power that, had Bill not given Charley a *'device'* to force the blast back into itself… in a sort of *'implosion'*… then *'Other-Time'* may not have survived, at all!
'Now,' Charley thought, 'it had only been sensible… and good, forward thinking… to set up another *'holding-location'*. If Blackthorne had survived, he would, then, have needed to be held, there.
Tom Dawson was always a careful man.'

'It was ironic, though…' he thought, now, '…that Blackthorne's son would be the one using it!'
If this was, in fact, where Danny, actually, was.

Found

Bill checked the coordinates of the *'holding-cell's location'…* before he, and Charley, *'stepped-out'* together.

They were *'stepping'* to *'Out-of-Time'…* to *'between-times'…* neither *'Other-Time'* nor *'Earth-Time'.* Also known as the *'void'.*

Great care had to be taken, in order not to be 'lost' when making such a *'step'.*

Danny was expecting… someone… and he hoped it would be Bill.

He hoped Bill would help him to see a way out of this, even though he couldn't, personally, see one… as yet.

"**Bill!**" Danny greeted his friend.

"Charley…"

He acknowledged Charley – but was wary of his presence.

Bill was shocked at Danny's appearance.

He was *wild-eyed* and *drawn,* from lack of sleep. He was also as *'tight as a bowstring'…* through worry and nervous energy.

"Don't worry, Danny!" Bill tried to reassure his friend. "Nobody knows that we're here. Charley guessed where you'd be and that we'd have another '*holding-cell*'... somewhere."

Danny nodded to Charley with respect.
He was amazing, he knew, for someone so young but he wondered...
"Am I... your *enemy*, now?" he asked Charley, "...and '*Other-Time's...* Like my '*father*' was!"
"No." said Charley, simply. "I don't think so."
Relief flashed across Danny's face... and hope.
"Can you see a way out of this?" Danny looked, hopefully, from one to the other.

Bill wanted, so much, to say yes... to give his friend some hope.
But he had no ideas.
Charley had been watching Danny – and 'listening' to his own '*feelings*'. He felt no '*wrongness*'... no '*negative feelings*' about Danny... and nothing of Blackthorne, at all!
"Danny..." he asked, gently, "...do you mind my asking what your '*abilities*' are?"

Danny sighed and lowered his head.
"I can *pick-up* on other people's '*abilities*' and have an '*awareness*' of their intentions... immediately...

though not really a 'mind-reader'… it helps in the 'Security-Team'. I'm an 'empath', too, and pretty good at 'surveillance' and 'electronics'… though not as good as Bill!" he added, with an attempt at a smile.
"Well, in that case… as an 'empath' and more… can you tell that I only mean to help you?"

Danny stared at Charley for a while and Charley left himself 'open' to his 'probing'.
"Yes, I believe you," he said, relaxing a little.
"Good! Now I can tell you, Danny – that, had you anything of your 'father' about you, you could not have come, anywhere, near my mind. I would have felt any… 'wrongness' and would have 'repelled' you… as I did Blackthorne… and Savage!" Charley stated.
"I now, know, that you are no threat, at all, to 'Other-Time'!"

There was a relieved silence, from all three friends, for a while.

"Thank you, Charley," said Danny – and his words were heart-felt.
"But… what about the others?"
It was understandable that Danny should still feel fearful of the reception he might, well, receive from those wishing to protect 'Other-Time'.

"Ah, yes! Well, I have some thoughts, there.
It cannot be denied that you carry a different *'gene'*.
Your true father, as well as Philip and Delia, also
carried what we saw as the *'fractured-gene'*.
They were arrogant, unpleasant, self-important and
self-seeking but you are none of these things.
They were known of, since birth, and their DNA
tested and monitored. You were not!
Ethan Faversham was aware of you and that it was
thought you carried the same... *'altered-gene'*.
He didn't *know!*"

Charley was being led-on by his *'feelings'*...

"The other three were *encouraged* to be... *'different'*
and were all from very self-important backgrounds...
in *'Earth-Time'* that is.
You weren't. You were carrying Blackthorne's
'genes'... but also your mother's.
She is a credit to you. She *'shielded'* you... despite
what Blackthorne might have done to her... had he
known... had he found out! She brought you up to be
honest, kind, reliable and hardworking. She is both
brave and honest... as are you.
I believe you have inherited *'who you are'* from your
mother... and it is what you have from Stephanie
Bennett that has *'saved'* you... from what would have
been your *'father's legacy!*"

Danny's eyes shone bright with tears, here.

"Then... there's hope?" he spoke, desperately.

"**There is, Danny... Charley's right!**" shouted Bill –
who couldn't hide his own relief.

The three friends sat... drank *'Revite'*... and renewed
their friendship.

Charley suggested Bill stay with Danny whilst he
returned to discuss all that had happened, with the
'team'.

He also suggested Danny should get some sleep
whilst Bill was there with him.

Charley's Explanation

Charley *'stepped-in'* to Arnold's rooms.
He needed a word.

He asked Arnold to get the *'team'* together, including
his gran, with Dawson and Mickey from *'Security'*.
He also asked that SAM and Abi should not try to
'read his mind'. He asked to be *allowed* to explain
everything to them… before they made any decisions
or took any actions.
He told Arnold to ask them to trust him… again!

The *'team'* assembled in The Meadow – as Charley
had suggested.
Arnold told them that Charley needed to speak to
them all, urgently. He repeated what Charley had
asked of SAM and Abi – and asked that no action
should be taken… until Charley had finished his
explanation.

Dawson agreed to this… as did the *'team'*.
Charley's *'abilities'* were well known… and trusted.
When this was done, and agreed, Arnold *'stepped-
out'* to *'step'* back in with Charley.
They could see by his face that whatever this was
about, it was serious, and very important to Charley.

"Firstly…" Charley began, "…do you, all, still *'feel'* that I have a *'link'* to *'Other-Time'*? That, *'Other-Time'* and I *'co-exist'*… That, *'she'* allows me to do what is necessary… for her 'survival?"

The *'team'* were all in agreement with this.
They verified this to be the case… and Charley nodded.
"Then I will now explain why I *'needed'* to do… what I have done… and once you know 'all the facts', then you will decide what happens, next."

Charley drew a deep breath before he continued…

"I have found Danny…" he stated… waiting for their reactions.
"I will tell you where… when I have finished. Bill is with him, now, and he's asked me to tell you that, Mr. Dawson.
Bill is acting on behalf of his friend 'but' also as part of your *'Security-Team'*. He will not let Danny out of his sight."
Dawson nodded, relief etched across his face.

"Danny, as you can imagine, is over-tired and distraught.
He is hopefully, now, catching up on some sleep… with someone, he can trust, by his side.

Dawson would have interrupted, here, but SAM stepped in to allow Charley his say… as agreed. "Bill is with Danny, Tom… as Charley says. He is going, nowhere!"
Charley nodded 'thanks' to his grandfather and continued…

"I have '*felt*' that we were missing something.
I knew where Danny 'must' be and when I confronted Bill… he couldn't deny it.
He agreed… that, as I was going, anyway, to accompany me and later to stay with Danny, so that you would all know Danny was going nowhere and… so he could be a '*support*' to someone in, great, need.
I knew Danny was no Blackthorne or Philip Faversham.
Now I '*know*'!"
Charley saw his grandparents' understanding beginning to dawn on their faces.

"I opened my mind to him… and he could reach me.
I didn't need to '*repel*' him with the '*ability*' "*Other-Time*' has given me.
He is no threat!" Charley stated, clearly.
"When Ethan Faversham began his experiment in '*genetic-engineering*'… although misguided… he did

not do this to *destroy 'Other-Time'* but out of concern... he felt... for our *'evolution'*.

He never, actually, *'tested'* Danny's DNA ... he *'assumed'* it would be like the three that carried... what we have called the *'fractured-gene'*.

I believe he was wrong!

Stephanie Bennett was not a Faversham or a Blackthorne. She, and her ancestors were solid, trustworthy and hardworking. This is what she gave to her son... her *'genes'* and this is how she raised him to be. It is her DNA, which is prominent in Danny's *'evolved-gene'*.

I believe that, in Danny, the *'Other-Time-gene'* is different but... and this is the important point... it is not *'detrimental'* to *'Other-Time'* but advantageous! It is what Ethan Faversham *'hoped to achieve'*!

I believe Danny is part of *'Other-Time's' 'evolution'...* as I may be... and, after three failed attempts... Ethan Faversham's success!"

Charley gave a smile to Dorcas, here, whose eyes were welling with tears, for her *misguided* grandfather.

"Now..." said Charley, "...I believe Danny is no threat to *'Other-Time'*.

I have proven this... to myself. I suggest, now, that when he is rested... and with his permission... that

the *'mind-readers',* amongst us, should *'share'*
Danny's mind and prove, to your selves, that he is
innocent of any ill intent.
Prove that there is no Blackthorne waiting to jump out
at us and threaten *'Other-Time'*... again!
The *'gene'* he carries is not *detrimental* but could
strengthen us, in the future!"

The *"team'* looked around at each other, now.
Charley noted their understanding and their relief at
this news... both for *'Other-Time'* and for Danny.

'Team' Decision

"Where is he Charley?" Gran asked him.

Charley did not reply, not until both SAM and Dawson had assured him that they trusted his judgement and trusted Bill to take care of Danny - for now.

"He's *'Out-of-Time'*… in a new *'holding-cell-location'*. He needed time to think, so he put himself there, to give himself time and… *ironically…* where, he believed, you would, eventually, put him!"
"Poor lad!" Gran declared. **"He must have gone through hell!"**

SAM and Abi, it was agreed, would join minds with Danny, though at different times.
If they agreed with Charley's *assessment,* then it was suggested that Danny submit to thorough *'testing'* with the *'Medical Team'*.
Not only would this *ensure* his mind and body were well… and *'untainted'* by Blackthorne… but, also, to try and understand the *'evolved-gene'* that he carried. They needed to *monitor* its *development*, in Danny, and in his future descendants.

Dawson suggested informing Bill, that SAM and Dawson, himself, would visit Danny but only when he was well rested and up to talking.

He did this.

"Bill…" he said, before breaking contact, "…assure Danny that Charley has explained *everything*… and that everything *will be fine*. He has my word!"

Charley smiled with relief, as Dawson approached him to shake his hand.

"Once again, young man, I believe you've sorted out, what could have been, a very, unpleasant episode in our history.

I, for one, am very grateful to you… and, extremely, relieved. Danny didn't deserve all of this… and it took *you* to put everything into *perspective*.

Thank you, Charley.

SAM and Gran returned with Charley, that night, to Wisteria Cottage.

It seemed a long time since they'd all sat down, together, and just relaxed.

"You know… I really think I'm getting too old for all this!" SAM stated, between sips of tea.

"**Nonsense, dear!**" declared Gran, with a twinkle in her eyes.

"It's just this grandson of ours sees things so… clearly… and acts on them, too!" she said, with a slight reprimand in her voice, though not in her eyes.

"I just 'knew'… and 'Other-Time' didn't object.
So I 'acted'… with Bill…" he pointed out.
And when Danny 'probed' my mind… I was convinced I was right."
He smiled at his grandparents.
"Well, you 'saw' right to the heart of the problem…
That there, actually, wasn't one!" SAM sighed.
"You are quite… amazing, at times, Charley. To…"

He would have said more, here, but Charley interrupted…
With his own eyes twinkling, he said…
"Oh it's nothing really… it's all in the 'genes'!"

So, SAM and Gran relaxed.
They were extremely proud of their grandson.

Each sat with their thoughts and both thought of Henry.
They knew how very proud he would have been… was… of Charley, too!
Once more 'Other-Time' was free of threat and life was good.

Gran reached out for SAM's hand as they sat, happily, with their thoughts.

Colin Learns The Hard Way

Whilst all this had been happening in *'Other-Time'…*
Colin was also having a rough time.

Firstly he'd had to suffer some unpleasantness at the
hands of another 'Under 21's Team' player.
Ben Read had a 'following' amongst the older players
in United's Academy – and amongst the girls.
When Colin scored three goals in two matches… and
won the praise of the coach… Ben Read decided
he'd put Colin *'in his place'.*

"It's early days, Stubbs… just try and keep it up, eh?
You'll never stand the pressure!"
Colin was astounded! All his life he'd dreamed of
this… of playing for United'… and, now, he was
getting *grief* from his own team!
Over the next few weeks, other friends of Read also
cooled towards Colin.
Then, in the middle of a straightforward, training
session, he was tackled, badly, from behind and
received a very nasty, knee injury.

The doctors agreed with United's Medical Team – he
would be out of the team for several weeks.

Colin was desolate.
He knew it could have been worse but, he also knew,
however, that it was deliberate!
One of his own team had caused his injury…
deliberately!

He tried to talk to Leanne.
He'd seen her three or four times now… on what, he
supposed, were '*dates*'… though he was, usually,
with one or other of the team.
They'd met at a club, after a win. She stuck with him
…and he was flattered.
He'd introduced her to the team but, when he was
injured, she'd made excuses not to see him.
Now she was hanging around with Ben Read's crowd
and, what was worse, he caught her laughing at him,
after a comment Ben had made.

Colin was too miserable to talk to anyone… until
Charley rang and it all came out!

Charley went straight over to visit his friend.

"Honestly, Charley… I can't believe it!
It's all a nightmare! I've gone from living the dream…
to dreading turning up… even to train! Even seeing
the physio…

I live *in dread* of walking into Read or one of his
cronies! It's worse than being at school!"
"Tell you what, mate… since you're injured… how's
about you and me take a break? Get away from it all.
Can ask Bestie, too, if you like?
He'll have done at that *posh* school of his, now."

Colin was very tempted though he'd have to check it
out with his coach, and physio, the next day.
"Where'd we go, Charley?" Colin asked… getting
more enthusiastic by the minute. "Somewhere
warm… where girls will be sympathetic to an injured
footballer, eh?" he grinned.
Charley had to laugh.
Colin was, already, perking up, at the idea.

As he told Gran, later, however, it was getting away
from the club that Colin was, really, looking forward
to.
Just as he'd looked forward to getting away from
school… for years!

"That's very sad, Charley!
Colin doesn't deserve this! What did you say the lad,
behind all of this, was called?"
Charley told Gran all about Ben Read… but he didn't
know quite why she wanted to know.

Costa Colin

The three boys landed up in Spain.
It was sunny, full of Brits… so no language barrier…
and Colin was in his element from the second they
stepped (well 'hobbled' in Colin's case) off the plane.

They met up with other groups.
They were all there to have fun and, as Colin said,
"**To let yer bloomin' hair down!**"

Charley realised, quite quickly, that he'd also been in
need of a break, himself!

They messed around on the beach and jumped the
waves… until Bestie forgot himself and vaulted
several feet higher than anyone else… and the three
beat a hasty retreat back to the hotel!

Here they collapsed, laughed, drank coke… and wine
in the bedroom, at night.
That was until Colin, and Bestie, had one too many…
and they stuck to iced, fruit juices, and the like, from
then on. It was safest.
As Charley'd said…

"It's just too much trouble, keeping Colin from running, 'bopping' and even trying to 'fly' down the hotel steps on his injured knee… let alone stopping you…" (Bestie) "…trying to fly up them… in one jump!"

They met other groups… lads around their, own ages.
They played Pool with them or raced them, in the swimming pool, whilst Colin cheered them on and… on the last day, but one… they had visitors.

Abi and Dorcas *'stepped-in'* to their hotel, Pool Room.
They'd stayed in *'shadow'* until it was safe to *'appear'*.

Charley was, really, pleased to see them… especially Abi.
That was until she plonked a huge kiss on his lips and embarrassed him, big time, in front of the others.
Dorcas burst into giggles, immediately, and Colin just had to join in!

"No bloomin' snoggin' in the Pool Room… puts ya right off yer bloomin' game!"
"That's one of those 'Colin Rules'… is it!" Abi responded, dryly.

"Yes, sure is! Rules to abide by," Colin stated, in the most serious tone of voice he could manage. "Snogging is out… due to the large number of germs involved in the practice… especially 'Cooper Germs'… positively lethal!" he declared as Dorcas collapsed in giggles, once more.

"Anyway, I'm winning this blinkin' game… and you've grabbed my bloomin' opponent. Not cricket, that!" Colin continued.

"Poor dear!*"* said Dorcas, dramatically…

"It must be the sunstroke! He thinks he's playing cricket… at Lords!

Call the doctor… quick!" she declared.

"The two of you are, positively, 'bonkers'!" said Charley.

"Conkers?" Bestie joined in. **"No…it's not conkers… It's Pool!"**

"Oh dear!" groaned Abi

"Asses… one and all!"

Abi and Dorcas stayed for the rest of the evening, before *'stepping-out'* to be back in *'Other-Time'* for midnight.

They'd promised Arnold.

Charley was 'laughed-out'… and more relaxed than he'd been for a long time.

Abi had confided in Charley that both she, and SAM, had read Danny's mind.
They agreed with Charley that Danny was no threat to 'Other-Time'.

That was good news and, seeing Colin so relaxed and more like his old-self, was good, too.
He'd had a good night and a happy holiday and that was just what they'd all needed.

Meanwhile – Back At The Stadium

Charley knew that Colin was dreading returning to United's ground and to the *atmosphere* that he hated so much.
However – when he arrived – Read was nowhere around and the physio was really pleased with how Colin's injury was healing.

"Another week, Colin… and we'll have you back on 'light training' … at least." Alec informed him.
"You're a quick healer.
That's good!'

Alec Jones studied Colin – noting his body language and the way he'd look around, at every noise or passer-by.
"By the way, Colin… You've got real talent. It's been noted.
You're doing very well… and you might be interested to know… we're letting Ben Read go. Not the *'sort'* we want at this club.
You don't try and *'cripple'* your own team mates or try and gang up, on those with more ability, than you!
Good news, eh?" Alec grinned at the young man…
who might now be able to enjoy his football, again.

Colin was ecstatic!
He rang Charley and told him the news and all that
Alec Jones had said.

"**The 'Colin Stubbs Story'… begins here!**" he
ended dramatically.
"**Wally!**" replied Charley, laughing.
"Good luck with the training, though. That Alec, by the
way, sounds like a nice guy.
Someone to talk to?" suggested Charley.

Colin agreed and rang off, after promising tickets for
his next match.
"I'll get one for Dorcas, too," he'd said as an
afterthought. "She likes football. We had a nice chat,
that night in Spain."
Charley smiled.
After all, Dorcas was also a part of Colin's future.

Charley told Gran all about the holiday and about
how things had improved, for Colin, back at the
stadium.
"Mmmm, yes…" she said. "…Alec Jones always was
a nice lad. We were quite close in '*Other-Time*'… at
one time."
Gran returned Charley's stare… with a long, slow
wink!

Danny And The 'Team'

Danny was more than relieved when SAM, then Abi, both agreed with Charley that, despite his *father*, he was no threat to *'Other-Time'*.

Danny, actually, found himself as interested in his *'altered-genes'*, as the *'Other-Time Medics'* were. He, happily, took part in their physical and psychological tests and awaited the results, as eagerly as anyone.
The results were *interesting*.

Physically, Danny was, extremely, healthy.
He had extra *'strength'*… in that he could *'endure'* for much longer than the average. He could run, for longer, keep focused, longer, go without rest, or even without sleep, for longer and his eyesight and hearing were beyond the best the medics had, ever, known, None of this was news to Danny.
His *'team'* had come to recognise, early on, that he was the first to 'make something out', at a distance and to move quicker, with greater *endurance*, than any other *'team'* member. Danny was the one to do the, extra, hours of *'surveillance'*, without any ill effects, and, at times, with little, or no, sleep.

So the *'altered-gene'* improved *strength* and
endurance.

Mentally – Danny was a quick learner.
He had exceptional ability. His IQ was *extremely*
high. He learnt languages, easily, took on board new
concepts, with no problem, and was extremely *logical*
in his thinking.
All of this had made him an excellent member of
Dawson's *'Security Team'*.
So *'heightened intelligence'* seemed a possible factor
with the *'evolved-gene'* also.

As the *'medics'* and the *'psychologists'* were quick to
point out, however, all of this might be *'individual'*.
Just Danny's own *'abilities'* within *'Other-Time'*… and
further investigations of Danny, and his children,
would be necessary to back up the *'findings'*.

What Danny had always known, however, was that
he was *different,* somehow.
From childhood, he had always been able to make
the *right decisions*, find the *right answers* and keep
himself awake, all night… if he felt like it… without
any ill effects.
And, as well as this, he had never, ever, been ill… all
through his life!

He'd never had a toothache or a headache. He was 'super-fit'… with a fitness that didn't need *training,* or any exercise, to achieve.

Danny had told Bill and Charley all of this and that he'd obviously known that this made him 'different' to the 'norm'.
This was because of these '*abilities*' but, as the '*medics*' said, all of these things *might* be merely his, own, '*abilities*'… just as natural to him as '*shape-changing*' was to Arnold and '*travelling*' to Charley.

What he didn't tell them… was that he had a heightened sense of '*self-awareness*'… not a wish for power or *self-aggrandisement*' but just of his own *worth* and his *place* within his world.
He knew, however, that he would, always, fight for his own *preservation.*
'*Who wouldn't though?*' he'd thought.

But, if Charley hadn't come to his aid and fought Danny's corner, he knew he would have found a way to *avoid 'Other-Time's'* judgements and to *preserve* his '*abilities*'… no matter what!
He did not crave power, as his '*father*' had, but Danny Mason was one to win out in the end… he was, simply, a *survivor!*

If the time ever came, that he was needed in *'Other-Time'* to 'lead'… as a Dawson, say, or a SAM… he would be more than adequate to the task. He would be a *'leader'*… if *'Other-Time'* ever needed one.

Danny told himself, that this wasn't like 'Blackthorne'. He would 'lead'… when the time was right… because he *was* able… and more than capable of doing so.
This was not because he wanted *power…* or people to 'fear' him… but just because he could.

Abi's Disappointment

Abi was sat in The Meadow, contemplating… when Charley *'stepped-in'*.

"Hi, Abs," he said, smiling and producing a bouquet of multi-coloured roses from behind his back.
"Just for you… with love from me."

"Who told you?" she replied, stiffly… making no attempt to take the flowers.
" Arnold…?"
"No!" Charley declared, immediately aware and sensitive to Abi's mood.
He also knew that it was no good trying to keep the truth from her… she'd only *'read'* the truth in his mind, after all!
"No… not Arnold… Gran…
But Arnold reminded her… to remind me," he admitted, with a *lame* smile.
"Sorry, Abi! This Danny business… sort of filled my head."
"Yes, it would," she said, tartly, "…whereas by birthday… wouldn't have even entered it!" she retorted and *'stepped-out'*.

"**Oh-oh!**" said Arnold *'stepping-in'*… even as Abi *'stepped-out'*.
"By the looks of you… you've been *Abi'ed*!
I thought I'd hang back… until she'd gone!"

Arnold patted Charley's back, in a show of sympathy.
"Lesson learnt, eh? Never forget your girlfriend's birthday… especially if it's Abi!"
"**Good grief!**" groaned Charley. "**It's not as if nothing's been going on, around here! Is it?**"
Sometimes Abi could be, so, difficult!

"Anyway… how's things with you?" he asked Arnold, in an attempt to forget the last few minutes.
"Oh… you know… fair to middling… sums it up. Can't complain," Arnold mumbled.
He'd never been one for 'small talk'.

At that moment - SAM *'stepped-in'*.

"Oh… found you both together… good!" he said, sounding distracted.
"Just had a visit from Dawson. There's been some sort of *'incident'*… down by The Lake. Whole area's to be cordoned off, until further notice!" he informed them. "I'll let you know more, as soon as Dawson gets back in touch.

Oh, and Charley will you *'step-out'* and tell your gran?
I ought to hang around here."

Charley, immediately, *'stepped-out'...* and *'stepped-in'* to Wisteria Cottage.
He passed on SAM's message and sat down with Gran for a cuppa.

"So... how'd it go, with Abi?" she asked.

Gran listened... and wasn't at all surprised.
"Disappointment... that's what it is. She may understand the reasons *why* you forgot but she'll still be disappointed that you did.
It makes you a little... less than perfect."
"**Oh, great!**
Oh, well... you might as well have these, then, Gran!" said Charley, handing over the bouquet he still held in his hand... once again.

Abi *'stepped-out'* of The Meadow and away from Charley.
She *'stepped-in'* to the area around The Lake, once *'Sector 12'...* to sit, think and sort out her *'feelings'.*

Well, that was her intention.

However, when Abi looked around her, she realised that The Lake was not the *'beautiful area'* it had been, just weeks ago.

She was shocked.

The edges of The Lake itself, were covered, by a grey-green… goo! Abi didn't know what else to call it.

It looked sludgy, stagnant and, decidedly, unhealthy!

Looking about, she realised that the land around seemed to be covered by a low-lying, dank and dark mist.

The air felt unhealthy, too, thickly heavy and difficult to breathe.

'Menacing!' she thought… well she *'felt'* it, too.

And, although, she knew, she should *'step-out'*… she found herself walking towards The Lake itself.

Abi knew she was doing this… knew she shouldn't… she wanted to *'step-out'* and find the *'team'* but, still, she moved towards the water!

As she got closer she noticed how 'black' The Lake seemed.

Deeply black… with a *thick* blackness…

'Like the cellar…' she thought, *'at The Lodge…'*

The Lodge where Savage had held her, powerless!

She thought all this but still she moved towards its *'depths'* and, as she approached, she saw the *'tendrils'* break through the surface of the water and begin to slide, sinuously, towards her.

The last thought, in Abi's mind, was that she could hear screaming…

Securing 'Sector 12'

Dawson's *'Security-Team'* had *'gowned-up'* to enter the area.

Their information was that three people had disappeared, from the surrounding area, in the last couple of days and a fourth had been found *'raving'* about The Lake having died and that it had *'scared him'*… somehow.

Though he was able to tell them this, he had then collapsed and been, almost, *'catatonic'* since.

No one could get through to him, at all!

Bill and Danny were first on the scene.

Bill's *'Gizmo'* went crazy… the second they *'stepped-in'* and they were immediately *alerted*!

Something was, very, wrong.

Then Danny *felt* it, too!

It was Danny who saw Abi first, as she *'stepped-in'* and he pointed to her… just as Bill *warned* him that they needed to leave… now!

Danny was about to argue, as something flashed before his eyes!

The next second Abi was gone!

All Danny saw, as he *'stepped-out'* with Bill, were black *'shadows'*, that seemed to weave and wave above the water before, they too, disappeared.
It didn't really bother him, though!

The *'Security-Team'* then set up the cordon, in the form of an *'energy-shield'…* around the whole area… and sent for Dawson.

The *'Scientists'* were now studying the 'readings' *'Gizmo'* had taken, trying to make sense of them.
They reported to Dawson that the whole area was *'toxic'*. The *'fumes'*, from The Lake, they said, were *'emitted'* by the *'algae'…* never before seen in *'Other-Time'*.
It was confirmed that this would be poisonous to life and that a way had to be found to destroy it and as soon as possible!

Bill had returned feeling, violently, ill.
He was sick, hot and giddy… and he was, immediately, quarantined.

Danny was *'decontaminated'* before he was allowed to move amongst the rest of the *'team'*.
But then Danny, as they all knew, was never ill.

What A Birthday!

As Gran and Charley were drinking their tea, Dorcas *'stepped-in'* to inform them that the situation, in *'Other-Time'*, was now much worse and that they had all been called-in, to Dawson's office.

The three of them *'stepped-in'* together, as Arnold and Mickey were giving out the *'Revite'* and just before SAM *'stepped-in'* with a very anxious looking, Bestie.

Dawson was the first to speak.

"You may have heard that The Lake… now being referred to as *'Sector 12'* again, during this crisis, has been *'sealed-off'*.
This is true. Bill and Danny have secured an "*energy-shield'*, around it.
No one can enter and… what's more important… nothing can get out!
The whole area has been *'blighted'* again but, this time, it is *'confined'* to the area, itself, which has become *'toxic'* to all life!

Three people, it would seem, have disappeared within the area, over the last few days and another, a *survivor*… has also been effected… but is in no state to tell us anything!

Now matters are worse.
Bill has been quarantined. He has become ill since leaving the area and despite wearing protective clothing.
Danny, who was with him, has, as yet, shown no sign of illness but, being Danny, he probably won't!

Dawson paused a moment before adding…
We also have had a 'sighting' of Abi, within the area, but Danny said she '*stepped-out*'."
Dawson, having completed his report, now handed over to SAM who, they all realised, had more bad news.

"I am sorry to confirm that it was, indeed, Abi who Danny saw in the area.
She did not '*step-out*', however, she was '*taken out*'… by Bestie here… at speed!
That was why Danny thought she'd '*stepped-out*' and it is, I believe, why Abi is alive at this moment!"

Bestie explained that he'd used his '*inner-eye*' to find Abi, so that he could '*step-in*' and wish her a Happy Birthday.

What he saw was Abi, being drawn towards The Lake's edge and 'black arms'… *'tendrils'*… he corrected (looking at SAM) moving towards her.
"She was screaming… and I *'stepped-out'* of *'Earth-Time'* to her position and grabbed her… just before…"
Bestie paused here…

"I'm pretty sure they didn't touch her…" he finished, looking towards Charley, for the first time.
"No-one can visit Abi… or Bill… for now.
They are under strict *quarantine* until we know, exactly, what we're dealing with.

Charley was distraught.
If only he'd remembered… then Abi would have been safe… and well… now!

What a birthday!

'Sector 12' – Survives

Somehow the *'entity'*… that had once threatened *'Sector 12'* and *'Other-time'* had survived.
But how?

Charley and the *'team'* went through all that had happened.

Charley *'knew'* that Bill's 'destructive device'…
another *'gizmo'* as he'd called it… had been dragged into the *'core'* of the *horror* that had been, what Charley had called, the *'Entity'*.
It had tried to drag Charley to its *'core'*, too… just as it now seemed to have tried to drag Abi… with those same, black *'tendrils'!*

Charley shuddered at the memory of what had happened that day but also for what had almost happened to Abi!
Abi – who now lay *comatose*, in quarantine, with Bill.

"If the *'Entity'* had been destroyed… and we know it had…" Charley thought, out loud, "…then how could it, just, re-appear?"

The Lake had filled the enormous crater… that the destruction of Blackthorne's *'creation'* had caused.

"Could a 'fragment'… a *'seed'* of the original… have been left behind?" Bestie queried.

The *'team'* found this, highly, unlikely.
"What we do know…" added Arnold, "…is that something *'deadly'* is in there, now!
We also know that it has killed… or *fed*, we believe… on three people and is responsible for three more being very ill and in quarantine!"

"I *'heard'* something…" Dorcas began, **"…in fact I've heard it twice, now!"**
Dorcas, who *'heard'* voices or sometimes *'saw'* the future did not always realise the significance of this, until later.
"It said…
*'**He returned!**'*
Nothing else*…* just that!"

"Blackthorne?" Bestie queried, to Dorcas' shrug.
"Returned… came back… Blackthorne came back… after that day! So, did he create another of… those things?" Arnold suggested.

"*It* was '*aware*'… and he had left it to… '*feed*'…"
Charley stated, thinking.
"Did he return to '*Sector 12*' after that day… after I'd
'*fed*' it Bill's '*device*'?
But then, The Lake would have been poisoned,
before now, surely!"

Once again, it seemed, a 'dead man'… a man sent to
his destruction through the '*void*'… was having an
effect on '*Other-Time*'!

The '*team*' didn't want to believe this!

Listening

SAM was, desperately, worried.

'Sector 12' had turned from the beautiful lake to a poisoned 'evil' force… much worse than it had been, before… and he didn't know just how long such a *'force'* could be *'contained'*.

The *'Science-Team'* were *standing by,* ready to collect *samples,* to search for a way to *'neutralise'* the area, again.
But this wasn't like the 'E*ntity'* had been.
It was a whole mass of water… the land around… and even the very air within 'Sector 12*'!*

Dawson shared his own concerns.
He was at this moment arranging the *'evacuation'* of the areas around… areas that had known nothing about what was happening, right beside them!
This was unlike before, when adjacent *'sectors'* had become *'blighted'*.
Then, Toby Thompson and Dorothy Pinkton of *'Sectors 11 and 13'* had come to him, aware of the problem… as the *'Entity'* had fed and drained the land's *'energies'*.

SAM called in Dorcas and Bestie.

"I need you to work together, though *secluded,* to 'listen' and 'look' for answers. Anything, at all, that could give us a clue as to what, on Earth, is happening!" SAM explained.

"Or what on 'Other-Time'!" Bestie corrected.

(SAM didn't respond to this… and Bestie, *really,* wished he'd not said it!)

"We need to know where 'this' has *appeared* from… seemingly from nowhere… and how it's happened? We need to know if there's someone behind it… and if so… who?

And what…" 'if anything', he thought to himself, "… we can do to stop it?"

Dorcas and Bestie nodded.

They moved to Dorcas' room, drank 'R*evite*', and 'listened'.

The only clue, as yet, were those two words…

'**He returned!**'.

SAM 'stepped-out' for a cup of tea, with Peg and Charley, at Wisteria Cottage.

"Any thoughts?" he asked them.

"He's back," Charley, quietly, confirmed his grandfather's fears.

"I don't know how... **I don't!**" Charley emphasised, in response his grandparents' look of expectation.
"**But ... he *is* back!**"
Charley looked up at his grandparent's faces.
"Who else would have the power to destroy, what was so beautiful, just days, before?"

SAM sighed.
It was impossible... he knew... for Blackthorne to have survived. But, even so, as Charley spoke, SAM too, began to believe that, '*he*' had *returned.*
Peg took SAM's hand, in a simple show of support and understanding.
She looked at Charley... knowing the '*torment*' he was under.

"**It was *'not'* your fault, Charley!**" she said, firmly.
"Abi... was being... Abi! She wasn't, really, angry with you... she was making her point, Charley.
She '*stepped*' to The Lake... as an area of beauty... that you both love... to think... or for you to follow her, perhaps... with your bouquet?" she suggested.
"But what's done, is done!
You can't turn back the clock, so..."

'***Oh but I can...!***' thought Charley.

And before either Gran, or SAM, could stop him… he *'stepped-out'*.

Gran looked at SAM, horrified.

They couldn't follow Charley – they couldn't help or stop him!
They couldn't go back in time… to *'turn back the clock'*!

Tell No-one

Peg was about to *'step-out'* with SAM, to Dawson's office… but SAM changed his mind.

"No, Peg!
Wait! Wait… a while!"
His mind was warning him to hold off… just a while… to give Charley time…
But for what?"

They had to think.
"If he's back, Peg… where is he? Who is he?"
Gran took on his meaning.
She sat back, slowly, in her chair and poured, them both, a second cup of tea.
Then SAM and Peg discussed all *the possibilities…*
and thought how Charley might be *'altering'* history at that very moment!
And Abi joined them…

"Charley says I have to wait here," she said, simply.
"I'm still a little annoyed with him, though.
I *was* going to The Lake to think… for a while."
She gave a knowing smile to Gran.

"So he'd know I was disappointed. But I'd have returned and forgiven him.
Don't see why it's *'so'* important, though... as he said it was... for me to come, here!"

Abi looked at them both... they'd said nothing.
She looked around...
"**Oh! You've got my flowers!**" she announced, smiling.
Gran looked at SAM – who returned her *look* and raised an eyebrow!
'I'll make us, all, a nice pot of tea... shall I?" she said, as she picked up the teapot and headed for the kitchen.

"What's going on?" Abi demanded.
She was *picking up* on thoughts... she didn't really want to hear... or to know!

'Security' buzzed Dawson.
"At the hospital, boss! Abigail Drew-Featherstone just disappeared!
Causing a right 'flap'! She was *'comatose'* ... so she didn't *'step-out'*!
Do we try and follow?"
Dawson looked up, at SAM, who had just then *'stepped-in'* to Dawson's office.

SAM shook his head in response to the 'Security Team's' query.

"No! Don't follow… I'll advise you, shortly.
How's Bill?" he asked as an afterthought.
"Seem's fine, boss.
Wants to 'step-out'… but they're still running tests."

Dawson broke contact and looked up at SAM… waiting for the explanation.
"Let it remain a mystery, Tom," SAM suggested.
"Charley?" Dawson queried… to SAM's nod of confirmation.
"Just you, myself and Peg, Tom," SAM outlined.
"No-one else… needs to know… at all!" he sighed.
"Not until we get some leads."

'Abi's in 'Earth-Time', with Peg…' SAM spoke to Tom's mind, now.
'And Charley hasn't, as yet, returned.'
Dawson took on board, here, Charley's attempt to try and find just 'what was going on' from the evidence he could gain from the past.
'If Danny 'sees' anything… now… he's mistaken!
If he 'insists'… then we don't know Abi's where-abouts.
Bestie is 'confused'…' he added, '…but I'm off to see him and Dorcas, next.
I'll set his mind at rest… but nothing more!'

'**SAM!**' Dawson '*mind-spoke*' before SAM could '*step-out*', '*Is it 'him'… again?*'
'*I would like to say, 'No', Tom… but something is definitely not right … again!*
I'll 'mind-speak' you… later.'

With that, SAM was gone and Dawson placed his head in his hands.
He didn't know how much more, of this, he could take!
What he did know was that, once again, they were relying on Charley!

What Does It Mean?

SAM caught Bestie, with Dorcas.
He needed to explain.

'*Hi, SAM...*' Bestie greeted his 'Senior Adept'.
'*I already know! Charley 'stepped-in' to tell me that,
'my bit of history'... at 'Sector 12' with Abi... has
changed.
He says she's safe?*'
Bestie looked to SAM for confirmation.
SAM nodded but said nothing.

Charley was putting things right... and he had even
warned them to '*mind-speak*' only.
Good! He was obviously thinking clearly.
'*Anything to report?*' he asked... looking from Bestie
to Dorcas.
'*Yes... but I don't know if it's any use... if it'll help.*'

Dorcas handed SAM her notes, also understanding
the need for silence... just in case.
Blackthorne had *eavesdropped,* before!

SAM glanced at the notes and read...

'When the past is put right… in the future.'
Florence Faversham.

SAM looked at Dorcas who nodded, silently.

'He will be the one.'
unknown.

'Watch out for the 'change'!'
(said with urgency)

'He must trust his 'feelings'!'
Florence Faversham.

SAM sighed… and looked to Bestie.
'I can't find him. I've looked!' Bestie said.
'I saw something, though …'
He was hesitant here and glanced at Dorcas, who
nodded, slowly, *'…from the future… I think.'*
Bestie handed SAM a note.
There was one word written on it.

SAM nodded, sadly.

'But… what can it mean?' Dorcas queried.
*'We would have known … Charley would have
known!'*

Abi Saved

"What did happen, Gran?" asked Abi… as SAM *'stepped-out'* to find Dawson.

Gran looked at Abi, carefully.
"Charley didn't say?" Gran queried.
"No… just that he was sorry… and that he'd never forget, again.
He stopped me *'stepping-out'*… but I was only going to The Lake-side. I love it there. I wasn't really cross…" Gran stopped her, there.
"I know. I told Charley."
She handed Abi a cup of tea and began to explain…

"Would I have died?" Abi asked, as Gran ended her explanation.
"You were, very, ill, Abi…" she confirmed, "…but I can't say."
"Charley went *'back in time'*… to save me!" she stated… tears welling in her eyes.
"That must be… the best… birthday present… ever!"

Abi could say no more.
Now she was worrying for Charley – instead of for herself!

"Now… we can't ask you, what you *'saw'*… or 'felt'…"
Gran began, "That might have been helpful.
But… you are safe… and that's all that matters," she
smiled.
"I believe, though, that what you 'saw'… or… 'felt'…
made you '*shut down*' your mind to protect yourself…
or to '*hide*' your '*feelings*' or '*knowledge*'… from
something… or someone.
You weren't poisoned by The Lake and Bestie
confirmed the *'tendrils'* did not touch you."
"Another '*knight in shining armour*'!
I must thank him, later," Abi spoke, still overawed by
all that might have… had… happened!

Abi was thoughtful.
"Charley says I must stay here. He made me
promise!"
Gran nodded.

Charley Holds Arnold To A Promise

Charley 'stepped-in' to Arnold's rooms.

He'd 'made-up' with Abi… sent her to Gran, at the cottage, and seen Bestie, to tell him that Abi was safe.
Now he was collecting 'Travel-Juice' from Arnold – to last him for a time.
He wasn't sure how long that might be.

Arnold gave Charley six, small, plastic pouches of juice in a holdall but insisted that Charley told him just what he intended.
"I'm not sure…" Charley had confessed. "I'm just letting 'Other-Time' choose where it sends me."
He looked at his friend.
"Arnold… if I don't come back… and they are worried… tell them that, for me.
But don't tell them, how worried I am?"

Arnold asked if he could help… in any way… but Charley just shrugged.
"Just be ready, Arnold… in case!" Charley said and 'stepped-out', with a half smile, that he hoped would ease Arnold's burden, a little.

Arnold had picked-up on how worried Charley, actually, was.

He was, extremely, worried, too!

Was '*Sector 12*' the beginning of the end for '*Other-Time*'?

If the threat had not been destroyed, last time, what could they do, now?

And if Blackthorne was back… if a part of him had survived, to grow strong again… what next?"

Arnold, like the rest of the *'team'*, in their own way, set himself to *rethinking* just what it was that they had all missed!

How could they handle the situation in '*Sector 12*' now?

And, if Blackthorne had survived… if he'd returned… where was he?

Who was he?

'Other-Time's Choice

Charley sat in the Meadow – alone.
He took out a *'Travel-Juice'* pouch from the holdall,
already hung safely around his neck.
In his hand, Charley held his father's special *'pebble'*
and, in his pocket, the phone Gran had given him.
This had already helped Charley, in the past.

Charley sipped at his *'Travel-Juice'…* calming his
mind.
He sipped and thought about his experiences in
'Sector 12'… and about Blackthorne.
Whilst he thought, he turned the *'pebble'* in his hand.

As though he'd been called, Pogs appeared beside
him and, as so often happened, Charley stroked the
dog, as he turned the *'pebble'*…
'Take care, Charley,' Pogs spoke to Charley's mind.
'I'll wait, here, for you.'
Charley smiled at Pogs – closed his eyes and…

Pogs lay alone in the Meadow.
He whined, quietly, dropped his head on to his paws
and settled, to wait.

Charley arrived… at Dawson's office!

He didn't know why he'd been sent here, of all
places!
But Charley was, immediately, on his guard… against
whatever he might find.
He didn't know *'when'* he was here, of course, not
yet.

He was just off the main office in Dawson's 'overnight'
room.
He'd once found Dawson sleeping here, when
'stepping-in' from Blackthorne's *'hideout'* in *'Out-of-
Time'*.

Charley became aware of voices in the office, on the
other side of the partially, opened door.
Charley concentrated on what was being said…

"You know you will do as I suggest, Tom – as usual!
Why do we have to have this tiresome charade…
every time? Just call the *'team'* in and tell them we
have a *'traitor'* in our midst!"
Charley's heart missed a beat! This was Blackthorne!
So he was now, at some time before he was *'blasted
to oblivion'*, in the *'void'*.

"I **won't** do this!" Dawson was adamant.

"He is one of the finest men *'Other-Time'* has ever known! No-one would believe it!"

Blackthorne laughed, maniacally.

'As he had before the end!' Charley thought, confused.

**"SAM *will* be seen as a *'traitor'*.
I have decided…"**

Rage, caused Charley to see red!
He *'heard'* his blood *'pounding'* in his ears and pain *'roared'* across his eyes… blinding him.
'Calm… Charley… calm…' he heard.
Quietly…the words *'seeped'* into his mind.

'Florence… it was Florence', he thought.
(Florence was Dorcas' grandmother who he'd met, once, when *'travelling'* into the past)

Charley knew he had to find out *'when'* this was happening.
He took a careful step towards the door… peeping around…
There he saw Dawson, looking grey-haired and quite ill.

Charley now knew he was some years in the future. But, if so, how was Blackthorne…

It was then Charley realised, that Tom Dawson had seen him.

"You shame the body you *inhabit*!" Dawson declared. **"Ha! He no longer exists. His mind could not defeat mine. He tried… He failed!**

When The Lake responded to my call… the power came back to me.
When I left it… I was *'re-empowered'* and *'whole'* and took the body my son had *'held'*… for me.
It was… you know… his sole purpose in life!
His mother had made him weak.
**She believed she had hidden him from me…
From me!"** he laughed.

**"When will you, ever, learn?
I am, never, fooled!
He was born for that very moment… the moment I took over his body… and his mind!"**

Charley saw the side of Danny's face… older now… and so very like his *'father's face'* at the same age.
'Oh, Danny!'
Charley's mind mourned his friend.

'I'm so, very, very sorry!'

"You are too confident in your '*abilities*', Patrick.
You may, yet, be defeated!"
"No... not now! Not now!" he repeated. "Maybe...
once... at first... but, once again, you underestimated
me... and now you suffer the consequences!"

Charley withdrew his head and quietly reached for his
'*Travel-Juice*'.
He never withdrew it...

Before Charley could do... anything... he '*travelled*'...

2nd Chance

Charley was back behind the wall in *'Sector 12'*.

He watched himself… this time, from *'shadow'*.
He stood, seemingly invisible, to the Charley who sat,
behind the wall, drinking *'Travel-Juice'*.

He looked around at the *'entity'*… as its *'tendrils'*
spread out, around it, reaching out across a *'blighted'*
land.
What was he supposed to see?
What had he missed last time… as the other
Charley?

He knew… he *'felt'*… that, *'Other-Time'* was trying to
tell him something.

The *'entity'* took his eye… drew his eye towards it…
as it had before.
But, now, his *'feelings'* told him, to look beyond it…

Charley did, just that.
He refused to be drawn by the power of the *'entity'*
and looked beyond…

But what was he looking at? There was nothing!
Nothing... except... way beyond it, in the far
distance... and, then, he *knew!*

As Charley *'stepped-out'...* his *'other self'* heard
Blackthorne's voice and turned to look over the
wall... again... at Blackthorne and his *'creation'.*
This time an *'organic-based weapon'.*
But, it was *still* a weapon!

Charley landed back in the Meadow, disorientated...
and thoroughly licked, in welcome.
Pogs showed his relief at Charley's safe return.

He struggled to pull a *'Travel-Juice'* from the holdall
and drank it down... closing his eyes and trying to get
his senses on an *'even keel'.*
Pogs, who'd sat back, now licked Charley's hand.
'Shall I fetch SAM?' the query sounded in Charley's
mind.
Charley sighed... exhausted.

"Yes, Pogs!
And Arnold and Dawson..." he added...
"But Pogs... say nothing about my *'travelling'* ... to
anyone... nor let anyone else know where I am... or
where *they* are going!"

'Yes, Charley… I shall 'mind-speak' your exact words to SAM.'

As Pogs *'stepped-out'*, Charley closed his eyes.
He was slowly recovering with the help of the *'Travel-Juice'*.

Charley took long, calming breaths as he waited for the others to arrive…

Why Didn't We See It Before?

"I have seen a *'future'*… that must not come to pass!"
he told the others.
"I saw you, Mr. Dawson, talking to Blackthorne – but
many years in the future."

SAM, Arnold and Dawson looked at each other.
Charley told them all that he'd heard… to a growing
dismay.
He told them all about Blackthorne knowing about
Danny, right from the first, and that he had been born
to provide Blackthorne with the *'body'* he would need
… one day.
"He said that, we *'always underestimate him.'*"

And they accepted that they *always* had!

He told them how Blackthorne was, effectively,
running 'Other-Time' and *using* Dawson as a
'figurehead' only.
"He still liked to hear his own voice, though…"
Charley continued, "…and, he said, we could have
defeated him… once… but not anymore!"

Looking at Dawson, Charley told him how, when he'd seen Charley by the office door, he'd tricked Blackthorne into speaking about the things *they* needed to know.

"You were preventing *'that future'* happening, Mr Dawson."

He thought Dawson *'needed'* to hear this… and he was right.

"Thank You, Charley!" he replied.
He was feeling very tired… and very old… all at once!

Dawson sighed, sick to heart, about what could have happened, might yet happen, to *'Other-Time'*!
"And, Charley," he continued, "…call me Tom."

"When could we have defeated him, Charley?" Arnold asked, now.
"I didn't know… *but then…* *'Other-Time'* sent me *back in time.*
I went back to *'Sector 12'…* at the time I destroyed the *'Entity'*.
I was there, again, watching myself… just before Blackthorne arrived to *'feed'* it… when it became *'self-aware',"* he explained.

"I had to *tear* my eyes away from it… to try and look around.
That's what it did… what it does! It '*wills*' you to look at it… to move towards it.
Anyway, I needed to look beyond it… to see if I'd missed… something… before.

My '*feelings*' told me to look beyond… and there was nothing… except… if I looked *way beyond*… into the distance… I saw… The Lodge!" Charley explained.
"The Lodge…" repeated SAM, thinking.
"Why didn't we think about it before?"
"Yes, the cellar!" Charley continued. "It was the same dense blackness… like the '*core*'… like his weapon, used on Peterson!
Could it be that the cellar… is the '*main core*' of the '*Entity*'… or another '*Entity*'?
Could this have *fed through* to '*Sector 12*' and then '*poisoned*' The Lake… when the time was right… when Blackthorne was strong enough?"

Charley knew he was right.

"So, you're saying… Blackthorne '*fed*' part of his mind… '*essence*'… into the main '*core*'… and he remained there… growing stronger… until he decided to come out, into '*Sector 12*'… now The Lake… and that is why it is… as it is!"

Arnold couldn't quite get his head around all of this…
but, then, who could?

"What about Danny?" Dawson queried.
"Blackthorne says he took over Danny's mind… when
'he' *entered* it.
I believe him.
If we can get to Danny… before Blackthorne enters
his mind…
But I don't know!" he admitted.

"We have missed so many opportunities… before!"
SAM stated.
"If we can rid ourselves of Blackthorne… before he
destroys Danny's mind… all well and good but, if not,
we rid ourselves of Danny!"
"It wouldn't be Danny, then, SAM," Charley said,
trying to relieve his grandfather's mind of the *'horror'*
of what he was saying… of killing a friend!
"He will be *'all Blackthorne'*… then," Charley recalled,
sadly.
"The Lake *responded* to his call," he said.
"It *'empowered'* him… and made him whole."

Arnold was shaking his head.
"There shouldn't have been enough… left in 'his'
mind… to do that! How is it possible?"
"How, indeed?" SAM agreed, "But he has…

He's done... the *'impossible'*... again!"

The Lodge

Bill insisted on joining Dawson, now he'd been released from quarantine.
Danny was left with the *'Security Team'…* in charge of guarding *'Sector 12's'* perimeter.

They 'caught Bill up', quickly, on all that had happened.
He was as eager as they to try and stop Blackthorne, before he could get to Danny.

So, they *'stepped-in'* to The Lodge… now an *'Other-Time'* Care Home - and into the basement.
The residents and staff, had been evacuated when the *'blight'* hit *'Sector 12'*, once more.
At least they could, now, work out what to do, without putting anyone else at risk.

Bill knew how to enter the cellar.
He had once used *'Gizmo'* to check out the *'wards'*, *'mental-trips'* and *'energy-pulses'* around the door that led into the cellar… alongside Danny.

This was when Victor Savage had held Abi here and when they had rescued her. They had all been happy to just *re-lock* the door… using *'Gizmo'*.
They'd locked it… and left it!

Now it was *'Gizmo'* that helped re-open the lock, once again.
Drawing a deep breath, it was Bill who opened the door… to reveal the *'deep and solid blackness'* that they remembered, so well.
"Gizmo' gave them light, until the switch on the cellar wall, that Savage had once used, could be located.
The light that now lit the cellar though, seemed to be 'swallowed-up', on its far side.

Charley and Bill moved across the floor towards this *'phenomenon'*.
After a few steps, Bill grabbed Charley's arm and they halted, in order to add extra light, again using 'Gizmo'.
As the beam hit the floor Bill gave warning!

"Tendrils!" he shouted to the others… as the beam fell upon a very, large 'tendril'…
"It appears to be dead."
"We can't be sure, Bill! " Dawson warned. **"Go with care!"**
They didn't need telling twice!

Charley was the first to see it!
"What the…
Look out, Bill!"
It was Charley's turn to grab Bill's arm and give
warning.

They all gathered as '*Gizmo*' showed them the '*core*'
of this '*Entity*'.

It lay open… as though opened from the inside, like a
'nest'… or a '*womb*'! Charley realised.
'*That was it!*'
That's where Blackthorne had been healing and
'*empowering*' himself, with the '*tendrils*' bringing
'*energy*' from The Lake and '*Sector 12*'.
It had surrounded him, protected him and fed him…
like a baby in the womb… until… it seemed… the
time was right for him to take over Danny's body.

"**He's already gone!**
We're too late to help Danny!" Bill declared,
obviously distressed.

Charley was wondering just why '*Other-Time*' had not
sent him here, before!
Then realisation dawned… and Bill saw it, too!

"It was when we… Danny and I… *'checked-out'* The Lake… when we were *'suited-up'*!
It must have been then… that, *'he'* got Danny!"

It made sense.
Danny had shown none of the symptoms, that Bill had suffered, from being in the proximity of The Lake and the *'blight'*… as Arnold pointed out.

'Gizmo' picked up no signs of life within the *'opened-core'* or the *'tendrils'* but they could clearly see where the *'tendrils'* had broken through the cellar walls, in the direction of The Lake.
The *'Entity'* had drained the energy from The Lake and surrounding area to *'feed'* its *'core'* and its own *'inventor'*… and right under their noses!

What Now?

The *'Science-Team'* moved towards The Lake.

Their *'readings'* had changed.
There seemed to be no *'menace'* nor any threat in the water, now, or in the air.
It was just a flat, dead area… devoid of any life at all!
Within this area the land was devoid of all *'energy'*.
The energy… the goodness… had been, literally, *'drained'* from the land, like before, when *'Sectors 11 and 13'* had been affected.

Danny hadn't stopped the *'team'* moving in… *he*'d known it was safe…
But then Danny would never actually make, any decisions, again!
Danny no longer existed.

Danny had fought a short, painful battle… as Blackthorne forced his way into a healthy, strong body and into Danny's mind.
The *'father'* killed the son and *'revelled'* in the feel of being a healthy, young man, again… and at being whole!

The mind that had made 'Danny' who he was… no longer existed.

'So, what now?' **he** had thought, calmly.

"What now?" Arnold asked.
"We find Danny and we've got Blackthorne!" Dawson stated.
"And as soon as possible!
We can't afford to lose him, again!"

They *'stepped-in'* at the perimeter of The Lake and the *'Science-Team'* told them of the change.
Their results showed all was *'dead'* but no longer dangerous.
"And the *'Security-Team'*?" Dawson asked, as neither Danny – nor any of the others from his *'team'* could be seen.
"*Stepped-out'* a while ago… soon as we gave the *'all-clear'*.

"Great! What now?" Bill asked.
Charley came up with the answer…
"We ask Bestie to find him!"

Charley, SAM, Dawson and Bill *'stepped-in'* to Dorcas' room.

Bestie was still there and they, both, seemed very relieved to see Charley.

"Dorcas '*saw*' you… in Dawson's office… with Danny! It's Blackthorne… isn't it?" he said, sadly.

Charley nodded and then realised…

"**It was you, Dorcas!** It was you told me to '*calm myself*'!

I thought it was 'Florence'… from the past! You sounded just like her!"

"She is," said SAM, simply.

They asked Bestie then, to find Danny with his '*inner-eye'…* which he did, immediately.

"He's in '*Earth-Time*'…

He's with Stephanie… Danny's mum!" he shouted with urgency, at what he'd seen.

"**With me!**" Dawson ordered.

And they '*stepped-out',* as one, and *stepped-in'* to Stephanie Mason's home.

Too Late!

Stephanie Mason was screaming and *'her son'* was laughing!
"Don't you know me, anymore, Steph?" Blackthorne was asking her, as he, cruelly, gripped her wrists.

Danny's mother seemed paralysed with shock, as the *'team'* *'stepped-in'…* as one.
Bestie used his *'speed'*, to grab and pull her away from Blackthorne – before he could react.
But Blackthorne, merely, laughed and *'stepped-out'…* before they could stop him.

"**He's at Sarah's, now!**
Danny's girlfriends… I think!" Bestie spoke, urgently.
"**Yes, I see their photographs!**"
"**No!**" Stephanie shouted, in turn… rousing herself from her shock.
"**No, it's ok! She's here! She's safe!**"

Stephanie moved towards a connecting door behind which Sarah stood, shocked and shaking… as was Danny's mother.

"Danny…?" Sarah sobbed, looking towards them all… not wanting to believe all that she'd heard.

"I'm, so, sorry, Sarah," Bill answered, quietly. "So, very, sorry!"

He led her to Danny's mum and *'stepped'* them both out, to a place of safety and care… for now.

Blackthorne was at Sarah's… looking for Danny's girlfriend.

'He' now knew, the *'team'* were *on to him* and would follow him… so he didn't linger.

'He' didn't really need these women… though 'hostages' were always of use.

He'd follow another plan.

When the *'team'* *'stepped-in'* to Sarah's home – Blackthorne was gone.

"**Too late!**' Dawson was frustrated and angry. "**Where now?**"

They all looked to Bestie, whose eyes lost focus, as he sought Blackthorne's next destination.

"**The Lodge!**" he declared, after a few moments. "**But take care! He knows we are following…**"

"And he's got hidden weapons!
I *saw…*" Dorcas gasped a warning to them all, as
she also '*stepped-in.*'

Charley looked at Bill, who'd now followed Dorcas
into Sarah's home.
He held out his hand for '*Gizmo*'.
The '*team's*' attention was still taken by Dorcas, as
Charley '*stepped-out*'!
'*Don't follow!*' Charley's words echoed in SAM's mind.

But, Bestie didn't hear this!

Dawson looked up at Bill.
"He's got '*Gizmo*'? He asked Bill for confirmation.
"On '*stun*'?"
Bill shook his head, slowly.

Charley's Shadow

Charley *'stepped-in'* to The Lodge and listened.
Everywhere was silent.

He moved, slowly, into the cellar… his *'feelings'* on alert.
His skin was *prickling* but the cellar was empty save for the latest, dead *'Entity'*.
Then, Charley's *'feelings'* whispered to his mind.
'He's in the bedroom'… where the hidden dragon is.'

Charley *knew* this room.
It was where he'd gone to retrieve Blackthorne's *'weapon'*… when he'd been sent back in time by the man, himself.
Charley didn't *'step-out'* though.
He took the stairs, as quietly as he could.
A *'shadow'*, however, was there before him.

Blackthorne *'stepped-in'* to his old bedroom… though it was much changed, now.
The enormous bed and tapestries were gone but the *'dragon'* door, of his safe, was there, still… empty now… *'they'* thought…

But then, *'they'* were such fools!

He had returned, before, from *'Out-of-Time'*... from a time when he had done some of his very, best work. Only *'he'* now knew the new combination.

Blackthorne retrieved a box from within a hidden compartment, that he opened by pressing parts of the safe's frame in combination.
He took out its contents and *caressed* the *'weapon'* within his hands, lovingly...
As he turned to face the door...

"**Cooper!**" he spoke loudly and with authority.
"**Stop hiding out there...**
Come in... and face me!"

An Ending

So arrogant was Blackthorne that he didn't even *point* the *'weapon'* at Charley.
He stood… as Danny… looking straight into Charley's eyes.

"Well, well… we meet again… as I knew we would.
You are so predictable, Cooper!
Ever the *'little hero'!* Intent on saving *'Other-Time'*…
and your *feeble-minded* friends.
You never seem to learn.

It is your turn… to die.
You know that, don't you?
SAM will not help you… nor Dawson.
He will work alongside me… from now on.

It is my *'destiny'!"* he continued,
"Danny will be the one to *lead* *'Other-Time'* from now on… you see.
He's become very able… and very reliable… in everyone's eyes.
Now, he has, also, become *extremely,* useful!"

Charley stared – at Danny.

He tried to see if there was *anything* left of his friend. He had so wanted *'Other-Time'* to send him *'back-in-time'*... to before Danny's mind had died... before his own *father* had *taken-over his* body.
'Why hadn't it?'

The answer came from a *'voice'* he'd thought he would never hear again!

'Because... he would always be a 'risk'... a possible threat to 'Other-Time', Charley.
Trust your 'feelings', son...
Watch-out for the **change***!'*

Blackthorne pointed the *'weapon'*...
"It seems that you and I will never reconcile our differences, Cooper.
A shame... we could have achieved... so much, together.

Now *'Abigail '* will need someone... to console her... at her *loss.*"
He smiled at Charley, here.
Danny... who once helped save her life... will *'support'* her... and she will be the *'mother'* to the *'next generation'*.

To further the 'evolving-gene'... that is!"

Charley was *beyond* anger.

"A *calmness* stole over him.
He felt cold and certain... as he pointed *'Gizmo'*...
releasing the beam, that would destroy!

In that same instant, Blackthorne too, activated his
'weapon' and watched for Charley's death!

Then things went wrong!
The *'weapon'* fired... but only as it flew from
Blackthorne's hand... and the door, beside Charley -
disintegrated!

The *'beam'* from *'Gizmo'* hit Danny in the centre of his
chest.
He looked amazed as he looked down... at the hole
Charley had made.

It was Danny who, now, asked Charley to help him.
It was Danny's voice... in pain... that called Charley's
name.

Charley watched him and heard Danny's cries!

The 'weapon' flew out from Blackthorne's hand, even as Bestie moved out of 'shadow'… 'flew high'… and caught it before it could fall.

He took in the 'blasted' door… Charley's horror… and heard Danny, pleading in pain…

Bestie pointed Blackthorne's own 'weapon'…
And Blackthorne – not Danny - died in an agony, that neither Bestie, nor Charley, would ever forget!

They watched an 'aura' surround Danny's body, as it seemed to collapse, in upon itself… before it, simply, 'blew-apart'… to nothing.

Charley and Bestie stood in the bedroom… in The Lodge… and looked at the spot where Danny's body had once been.

Charley's Summons

Charley sent out a *'mental summons'* to the *'team'*.

Now they all stood, together, within the bedroom of The Lodge... so large and grand that it held them all.

Bill, carefully, took Blackthorne's *'weapon'* from Bestie's hand.
Arnold *relieved* Charley of *'Gizmo'* and handed that back to Bill, also... once the *'weapon'* was *'sealed'* back within its box... safely.

SAM looked into Charley's eyes.
Eyes that still showed the horror of what he'd seen and that SAM, through Charley's mind, now saw, too.
He shared Charley's pain and helped cushion the shock... and Peg and Abi *'stepped-in'*.

They put their arms around Charley – as SAM stepped over to Bestie.
He would *'share'* his horror, too, and make his memories as bearable, as possible!

The *'team'* stood, reflecting.
"Blackthorne's gone!" Dawson said.

It was a statement, not a question. It was said to give some finality to their situation… a need to 'state' that it was all over… at last!

The threat was ended.

"And… Danny?" said Bill.
They heard the emotion in his voice. "He's… gone?"
Charley met his eyes… and nodded.
Charley could not speak or trust his voice… not yet!

He held hard to Abi's hand and put his other hand over Gran's – as she gripped his arm in support.

It was over.
But the relief that they had defeated Blackthorne could not *eclipse* the grief… the knowledge… that today they had lost a *'team'* member and a friend.

Danny had been born… his own father had said… to provide a body for Blackthorne.
That had been his, only, purpose.

"It was his *destiny,* also…" SAM stated," …to provide the means to destroy the *'father'*.

By *'taking over'* Danny's body and becoming *whole, again...* this made it possible for him to be killed, once and for all!"

Danny would always be *honoured* and *remembered* within the history of *'Other-Time'*.

Thinking Things Through

There was no easy way to break the news to Stephanie Mason.
Her son had died and there was no body left to mourn.

Danny had died beforehand, however, as she'd known... when Blackthorne had *'stepped-in'* to her home.

Both she, and Sarah, came to a short service... where people shared their memories of a trusted colleague, a valued *'team'* member and a loyal friend. That, *'Other-Time'* honoured Danny – made both mother, and girlfriend, very proud.

Bill consolled Sarah and took the two women, who Danny had loved so much, safely home.

"Bill will make her happy... and Stephanie will be pleased..." Dorcas announced, flatly, after they departed.

There was, then, something good to come out of all of this.

SAM, Arnold and Dawson spent a few hours in thought, reminiscing, but also thinking of the future.

"Soon…" said SAM, "…it will be time for the younger *'team-members'*… to run this shop!"
Dawson sighed…
"I know what you mean, SAM. I feel I've aged… beyond years… at times!
I, for one, am so, very, glad *'he'* has, finally, gone!"

Arnold chuckled.

**"Listen to you two!
A good night's rest and you'll soon be putting us all through our paces… again!**
Anyway…" he continued, " …you've still got another job to do!"
He looked at SAM.
" *'Sector 12'* " SAM guessed.
"**'*Sector 12'*!**" Dawson groaned. "**Give me a break… and a '*Revite*'!
Let's think about that, tomorrow!"**

Charley returned to Wisteria Cottage… to Gran and Abi.

Gran, tactfully, went to make the tea… shutting the door behind her.

"Thank you, Charley," Abi whispered.

He looked up and thought what it would have been like, if he'd lost her.

"You were my *'knight in shining armour'…* and you gave me the best, birthday present… I could ever have had!" she finished.
"Well, they're only flowers!" he stated, dumbly.

"Flowers…!
Well…!" she blustered.
"Here I am, trying to tell you what I feel… how much it means to me… and all I get… all I get…! Oh, you… you… absolute a…!"

Charley smiled, as she *'ranted'* at him… and cut off her words, with a kiss.

Suddenly, everything seemed all right, again.

He had Abi and Gran, SAM and the *'team'* and, for once, no Blackthorne!

Gran came through with the tea tray.
Now, we all need a nice cup of tea," she said.
"Everything seems much better…"
"**…after a nice cup of tea!**" Abi and Charley finished for her, smiling.

Life was good, again.

Loose Ends

Charley and Abi 'stepped-in' to The Meadow - to find
Bestie and Dorcas sat, quietly, together.

They stood up to greet them… relief showing on
Dorcas' face… that Abi was back and looking so well.

"I need to thank you, both," said Charley.
"Without you two… I might not have made it!"
"It's the least we could do, Charley," said Dorcas.
"I only helped you keep calm, anyway.
It was Bestie, here, who 'saved the day'… as it were!"

Charley turned to Bestie – who looked a little
sheepish.

"Thanks, Bestie… for everything," he said, simply.
"I'm so pleased that you didn't give up on the 'team'.
Without your 'Inner-Eye'… and 'acrobatics'… I
couldn't have got to Blackthorne, so quickly and…
then… he would have killed me!"

They all realised the truth of this.
And both Charley and Bestie shuddered thinking on
what they had witnessed… when Bestie had used the
'weapon'… on Blackthorne.

"You'd just about done for him, anyway… and when
he started using Danny's voice… you hesitated…
But my *'Inner-Eye'* couldn't find anything of Danny…
He was gone, Charley!
I saw, only, Blackthorne and he had to die… before
anyone else did!"

Bestie hesitated before continuing…
"It was hideous… but I'm not sorry I did it!"

Abi came up and kissed Bestie, here.
"Thank you for saving me at The Lake, Connel… and
thank you for not forgetting my birthday.
And thank you… again… for saving Charley.
I know I was cross with him… for forgetting my
birthday… but *'disintegration'…* would have been a
bit… harsh!" Abi finished, with tongue in cheek… and
that twinkle in her eye.

Connel Bestwood, laughing aloud, picked Abi 'up'
here… about six feet up, to be precise… and swung
her around until she was breathless!
Then he pushed her towards Charley…

"You're going to have your *'work cut out'* with this
one, Charley!" he declared, grinning.
"**Don't I know it!**" he replied, as he stepped away
from her 'well-aimed' elbow.

Then Arnold 'stepped-in' and informed them that
SAM wanted the 'team' at 'Sector 12'.

The change was easy to see as the 'team' 'stepped-in'… to sunshine.
The water in The Lake wasn't yet clear, blue and
inviting but neither was it grey and sludgy.
'Teams' were removing the 'tendrils'… now dead and
drying… and the 'Adepts' were ridding the area of its
recent 'infestation'.

SAM and Dawson were 'overseeing' the 'changes'
and they, both, seemed rested and more relaxed than
Charley had seen them, for quite some time.

Then Charley remembered what had happened,
before he'd shot Blackthorne with 'Gizmo'.

"There's something… I haven't told you, SAM…" he
said.
"Before I pointed 'Gizmo' at Blackthorne… at
Danny…
A voice told me that…
'**He** would always be a risk… a threat… and that I
should watch for the 'change'!'

Having repeated the words – Charley drew a deep breath…
"That gave me the strength to activate '*Gizmo*'.
The '*change*'… I believe… was when he used Danny's voice… when he was crying-out in pain… at what I'd done!
I didn't shoot again, though… I couldn't… despite the warning!
It was Bestie who did, what had to be done… to make sure!"

"Whose voice was it, Charley?" asked SAM.
Charley looked into his grandfather's eyes and said, proudly…
"It was Dad. Dad warned me.
He was with me!"
"Oh, Charley," SAM said, gently, as he gave his grandson a loving hug.
He was, very, proud, also.
"I'll tell Peg," he told Charley.

And Charley knew that this would be a '*special moment*'… for his grandparents to share.

Back To Normal

The Autumn Term was fast approaching.

Charley spent as much time as he could, before then, with the *'team'*... and Abi.

There was a new light-heartedness about *'Other-Time'*.
Life was back to normal, again.
They could look forward to the future... without looking over their shoulders.
There were no more threats.

Abi and Charley spent time, alone, in The Meadow or at The Lake - now re-emerging, once more, as the place they'd both enjoyed visiting.
There was now a different view, however.
The Lodge no longer existed.
There were just, too many, bad memories associated with it, to leave it standing.

Charley and Abi talked, briefly, about this next year – Charley's last at Broomhill School's, Sixth-Form College – and about what would happen, then.

He was, still, unsure.

He felt he'd come to *'Other-Time'* to continue his studies.
They had an excellent *'Science-Team'* and he was tempted.
Whatever happened, his *'double-life'* would continue, he knew. It was really a question of *where* he would be based?
He felt his future was with Abi, or so he hoped, but Abi wouldn't talk about the future, yet.

They were happy being in each other's company and amongst their friends and family.
Abi counted Charley's grandparents as her own and, of course, there was the *family* that was the *'team'*.

So, they relaxed and let the days pass by.
They appreciated being able to do this now and understood how *'precious'* such times were.

Colin, as promised, provided Charley with tickets for the next game, the first of the season, in the Reserve Team.
He asked Charley to give one to Dorcas.

"She said she'd like to see me play," he reminded Charley – and there was a spare ticket for Abi or Bestie.
As Bestie was on a last-minute break with his family, it was Abi who accompanied Charley and Dorcas.

Charley got the impression she was as interested in Colin and Dorcas – as she was in the game.

"**He's very good, isn't he?**" exclaimed Dorcas – as Colin's second goal hit the back of the net.
"I really don't know what the fuss is all about!" Abi declared.
"It's a little ball… and a very big net!
It can't be too hard to score… can it?"

Charley listened to their comments and smiled to himself.
He certainly knew how hard it was to score and he was proud of how Colin was doing.
He also enjoyed watching his friend and Dorcas, growing closer.

Though Dorcas was only fourteen… well, nearly fifteen now… they were so obviously *'taken'* with each other.

Colin *relaxed* around her and she... well, she
became one of the 'crowd'. The '*crowd*' being Colin,
Charley, Bestie, Abi and Dorcas.
By the time Colin was two or three years older and
Dorcas seventeen or eighteen, he would be
established in his career and Dorcas would be an
'A*dept'* with a '*huge house'...* of her own.
The house was 'Faversham Hall'... and she would
have all the *wealth* that went with it.

Yes, the future looked, very, bright for his friend.

When Colin hit the woodwork with his next attempt,
Dorcas was nearly *hoarse*, with the effort of shouting
her support.
Abi looked at Charley - and grinned.
"She's definitely *'smitten'*," Abi whispered.
"Your friend stands no chance!"

"She's just what he needs," Charley replied, quietly.
"And you... well, you're just what I need," he
continued, looking, very, serious for the moment.
Abi looked back at him, took his hand in hers, and
smiled.
"Ditto!" she responded, happily.

When Colin joined them after the game, Charley noted, again, how his friend was changing.

This Colin was fit, confident and very happy.
"I'm playing in the 1st Team… again… next week. Impressed 'em all today… apparently!"
"**You were wonderful, Colin!**" Dorcas enthused.
"Oh… thanks!" Colin said, beaming.
"So, whose for pizza, then?" he added, with a grin.

"**Wow!
What a surprise!
Colin fancies pizza!**" Abi declared, dryly… though she grinned at Colin.

"I'd love pizza, Colin…" said Dorcas.
"**Then your wish shall be granted… dear heart… Lead on!**" he added, dramatically.
"**I'm bloomin' ravenous!**"

Dorcas walked alongside him, giggling with pleasure. Abi looked up to heaven!
"**Good grief!**" she said to Charley.
"**We've got years of this, before us! It's painful!**"
"**No…**" he answered. "…**its great, Abi!
Just great!**"

And, with that, Charley put his arm around Abi and they followed along behind Colin… who was in 'full flow'… and Dorcas who hung on his every word… grinning, happily.

Find out

Where Charley's next Adventure leads him…

Now that Blackthorne has, finally, gone.

Read:

Charley Cooper

'Lost In Time'

Read also

'Hoppers'

'Golden Brook'

'Guardian'
Gift

&

<u>**NEW**</u>

'FireLands'

(A Trilogy)